For Mikey x ~ RV

Princess Natalie and Prince Michael! ~ EE

Bloomsbury Publishing, London, Oxford, New York, New Dehli and Sydney

First published in Great Britain in 2016 by Bloomsbury Publishing Plc
50 Bedford Square, London, WC1B 3DP

Text copyright © Rachel Valentine 2016
Illustrations copyright © Ed Eaves 2016

The moral rights of the author and illustrator have been asserted

A CIP catalogue record for this book is available from the British Library

ISBN 978 1 4088 6265 0 (HB)
ISBN 978 1 4088 6266 7 (PB)
ISBN 978 1 4088 6264 3 (eBook)

Printed in China by Leo Paper Products, Heshan, Guangdong

1 3 5 7 9 10 8 6 4 2

All papers used by Bloomsbury Publishing are natural, recyclable products
made from wood grown in well-managed forests.
The manufacturing processes conform to the environmental regulations of the country of origin

www.bloomsbury.com

BLOOMSBURY is a registered trademark of Bloomsbury Publishing Plc

Marmaduke
the Very Popular
Dragon

Rachel Valentine

Ed Eaves

BLOOMSBURY

LONDON OXFORD NEW YORK NEW DELHI SYDNEY

Marmaduke and Meg were different.
Brilliantly, happily different.

They were best friends, and they were always together: practising Whizz Cone, having adventures or sneaking off to their secret spot on Wispy Mountain.

Everyone else would watch Marmaduke and Meg.
They **wished** they could have that much fun.
But . . .

. . . the princesses sat in their towers.
And the dragons stood guard.
Because that's how it had **always** been.
Until . . .

. . . the day one princess decided to be brave.
Princess October walked quietly up to Marmaduke and Meg.
"Could I play with you?" she whispered.
"Absolutely!" said Marmaduke.

And soon October was having more fun than she'd ever had.
Slowly, slowly, word spread across the kingdom.

First the other princesses joined in.
Then the dragons. Then the princes. Even the knights.
The kingdom became a happy place.

Marmaduke had never had friends before, apart from Meg,
but now **everyone** loved him and his amazing wings.
It felt wonderful being so popular, and he was always busy

helping Ockie with fire breathing,

toadstool snuffling with Princess Penny,

teaching Whizz Cone to Prince Bertie.

Meg barely saw her friend, but she was
pleased that Marmaduke was so happy.

"Just don't forget the tournament," she said.
"Never!" said Marmaduke.

WHIZZ CONE

TOURNAMENT

The king had decided to hold a Whizz Cone Tournament.
Teams from near and far would battle for the Golden
Whizz Cone Cup. Each team had a dragon and rider,
perfect for best friends like Marmaduke and Meg.

Soon preparations for the tournament began.
There was great excitement as garlands were strung
from tree to tree and banners flown high.

But as Meg sat alone, watching the royal flag
being raised, she thought sadly, *It would have been
much more fun to watch with Marmaduke.*
She decided to look for him.

Marmaduke wasn't in his cave.

He wasn't in the toyshop.

Or even the ice-cream parlour.

I know! thought Meg. *Wispy Mountain!*
She skipped to their secret place . . .

. . . but as she got closer she heard voices.

Marmaduke **was** there, with Prince Bertie, who was laughing,
"Thanks for asking me to be your partner, Marmaduke,
I'm SO excited about the Whizz Cone Tournament!"
"Me too!" said Marmaduke.

Meg gasped. She and Marmaduke
always played together . . .

. . . he seemed to be forgetting about her.
Before they could see, Meg crept away.

At last it was the Whizz Cone Tournament, and the whole kingdom had come to watch. The gong boomed, the pine cone was flung and the games began! Riders whipped the cone from their rivals and hurled it through goals. Dragons spun and dived, and the crowd roared:

"Marmaduke! Marmaduke! Marmaduke!"
He was their favourite, and he and
Bertie were playing brilliantly.

But Meg found she didn't want to
watch them scoring goal after goal.
Quietly, sadly, she slipped away.

The Whizz Cone teams battled on all afternoon, until the final gong.
And then the winners were announced.
"In first place, with 55 goals . . .
. . . Marmaduke and Prince Bertie!"

Grinning, they collected the enormous Golden Whizz Cone Cup.
Everyone crowded around, congratulating them and cheering.
And Marmaduke **should** have been happy . . .

. . . except something was missing.

Suddenly he realised . . . Meg was missing!

Marmaduke wriggled away from the crowds and pricked up his
enormous ears. From far away, he heard the sound of sobbing.

"Meg!" he called, soaring to the sky.

But as he flew towards the sobs, Marmaduke had a **very** uncomfortable thought, *I have **not** been a good friend to Meg. I haven't spent any time with her.* Then he gulped. *And I left her out of the tournament!*

From up high Marmaduke spotted Meg
sitting alone on Wispy Mountain.
He dived down.

"I'm really SORRY Meg.
I was so busy with my new friends,
I forgot about my best friend."

"I did feel left out," said Meg quietly, wiping away a tear.
"I'll never, ever do that again," Marmaduke promised,
scrunching her in a huge hug.

And from that day, Marmaduke kept his promise.
No matter how many friends he and Meg had . . .

. . . Marmaduke **always** tried his hardest to be a **good** friend.

"And a good friend," beamed Meg,
"is the **very** best thing in the world!"